This book belongs to

conal

Fun-to-Read Picture Books have been grouped into three approximate readability levels by Bernice and Cliff Moon. Yellow books are suitable for beginners; red books for readers acquiring first fluency; blue books for more advanced readers.

This book has been assessed as Stage 4 according to *Individualised Reading*, by Bernice and Cliff Moon, published by The Centre for the Teaching of Reading, University of Reading School of Education.

First published 1986 by
Walker Books Ltd
184-192 Drummond Street
London NW1 3HP

First printed 1986
Printed and bound by
L.E.G.O., Vicenza, Italy

British Library Cataloguing in Publication Data
West, Colin
'Pardon?' said the giraffe. – (Fun-to-read picture books)
I. Title   II. Series
823'.914[J]   PZ7
ISBN 0-7445-0525-9

'Pardon?'
said the giraffe

Written and illustrated by
Colin West

WALKER BOOKS
LONDON

'What's it like up there?'
asked the frog
as he hopped on the ground.

'Pardon?'
said the
giraffe.

'What's it like up there?'
asked the frog
as he hopped on the lion.

'Pardon?' said the giraffe.

'What's it like up there?'
asked the frog
as he hopped on the hippo.

'Pardon?' said the giraffe.

'What's it like up there?'
asked the frog
as he hopped on the elephant.

'Pardon?'
said the
giraffe.

'What's it like up there?'
asked the frog
as he hopped on the giraffe.

'It's nice up here, thank you,'
said the giraffe,
'but you're tickling my nose
and I think I'm going to...'

A-A-A-TISHOOOO

'What's it like down there?'
asked the giraffe.

'Pardon?'
said the
frog.